Jesus Says:

You Are The Light Of The World.

Judith Tamasang Jogwuia
Illustrated by Mukah Ispahani

Note to Parents and Guardians:

Dear Parent or Guardian,

This book is designed to introduce Jesus Christ to young readers in a simple and nurturing way, focusing on His love and the importance of using God-given talents to let one's light shine. Featuring engaging prayers and Bible verses woven into personal affirmations, it aims to inspire children with faith and confidence while grounding them in biblical wisdom.

Every time you read this book, you plant the seed of Jesus in your child's heart, trusting that, in time, He will fully reveal Himself as they discover and walk in their God-given purpose. The 'Jesus Says' affirmations repeated throughout the book will echo in their spirit, helping them grow in their identity in God.

Like Jesus, may your child grow in wisdom, stature, and favor, walking confidently in the knowledge of His love and God's plans for them. We pray that not only will they discover their gifts early, but that you will nurture them so their light shines brighter, drawing many to Christ.

May this be your child's legacy. May the seeds you plant today bear much fruit in their life. In Jesus' name, we pray. Amen.

Described as a soothing guide for young souls, this book is filled with positivity and rooted in Christian values. It is perfect for parents who want to raise their children with a solid spiritual foundation and a strong sense of identity and faith. It can also be used in Sunday school classes or as a bedtime devotional for families.

Thank you for the great privilege to be a part of your child's spiritual journey.

Lots of Love,
Judith Tamasang Jogwuia

Jesus says: You are the Light of the world!
A ray of sunshine to light up a dark world,
Like the morning sun, your star arises...
To light up the world's stage,

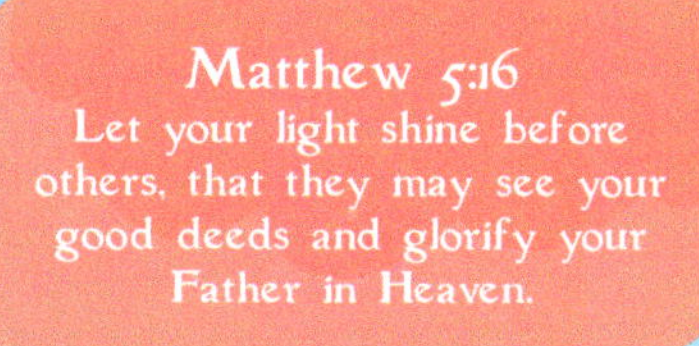

And bring hope to people.
For a people in darkness will see,
The Great Light of Jesus through you,
As all darkness gives way to the
brightness of your light.

Prayer: Dear Lord Jesus, bring out my light so the world can praise you.

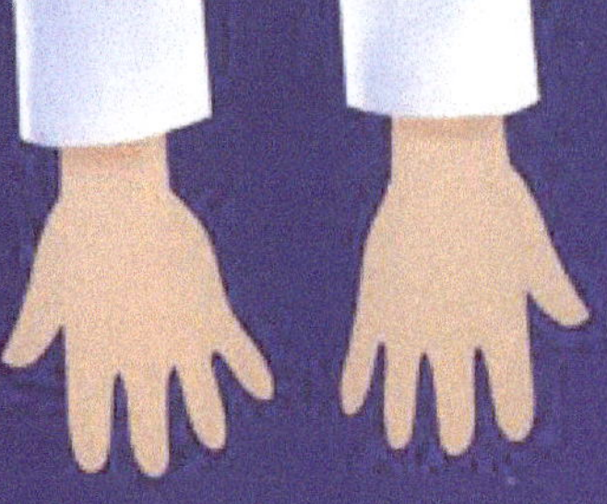

Jesus says: You are the Light of
the world!
A tiny acorn seed waiting to
grow into a very big tree.
From the beginning of time, God
created you special.
Out of the darkness, the Lord
formed one copy of you only.

Into your mother's womb, He placed
you for a purpose.
On the day you were born, there was
joy in Heaven.
The world eagerly awaits to see you,
my darling.

Prayer: Dear Lord Jesus, I am Your child. Let Your light shine through me.

4

Jesus says: You are the Light of the world!
A rare gem in our Father's big hands,
Your rainbow colors shall glow
And cut through the darkness all around.

Just one squeezy hug—and all sadness is
melted by your love.
Your radiant smile lights up the world,
Bringing lost hope back to life.
A bundle of joy you are, my darling.
How I love you so!

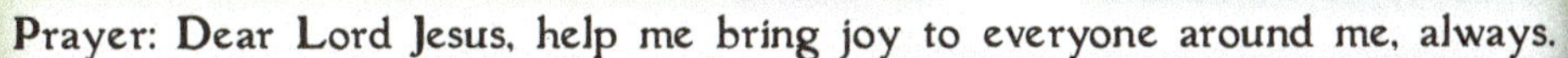

Prayer: Dear Lord Jesus, help me bring joy to everyone around me, always.

Jesus says: You are the Light of
the world!
A city built on top of a hill
cannot be hidden.
Like a lighthouse, your beams
will shine stronger each day,
And bring ships in troubled
waters safely to shore.

Nations shall be drawn to the
beauty of God through your light,
As your good works draw the
world to Jesus.
Not for fame or gain,
But to spread the love of Jesus
Christ to everyone, young and old.

Prayer: Dear Lord Jesus, let your light in me draw people closer to You.

Jesus says: You are the Light
of the world!
Your light cannot be hidden or
dimmed, forever.

Darkness tries and fails every time
To stop your glorious swirl or smile.

Prayer: Dear Lord Jesus, You are my Everlasting Light. Guide me every day of my life.

Jesus says: You are the Light of
the world!
When storms rock the boat of
your life,
They too will surely pass, in time.
Through the journey, be strong
and courageous,
Patiently trusting that you are
never alone.

Our Lord Jesus is always near!
Just be still and whisper His
name—JESUS!
And the Prince of Peace will
appear and calm your storm.
Like Noah, Captain Jesus will lead
your boat safely to shore.

Prayer: Dear Lord Jesus, teach me how to trust You through the storms of life.

Jesus says: You are the Light of
the world!
When dogs and werewolves
surround you,
And the night seems so long that
comfort seems far from you,
Do not fear, my darling—Jesus is
always near.

Prayer: Dear Lord Jesus, wrap me safely in your arms and guide me with Your wisdom.

Jesus says: You are the Light of
the world!
When life is tough and you can't
seem to find a way out,
Remember that Jesus holds your
life in His safe hands.
Just call His name—JESUS!

And the Way Maker will bring
springs to water your desert.
He will stir up your creative gift
to break forth like the morning
dawn.
If you keep trusting in Him, Jesus
will make a way for you
Whenever you can't find one.

Prayer: Dear Lord Jesus, I trust that You will make a way for me whenever I feel lost.

Jesus says: You are the Light of the world!
God's own special treasure, carefully and
beautifully made.
As Jesus watches over you, He smiles at your
beauty.
Your gifts shall make room for you, my
darling.

Kings and nobles shall come to see
your beauty,
For the Light of Jesus shall arise
from within you.
Born to be fruitful and great—you
shall prosper!
Jesus will prepare a feast for you
amid your foes.

Prayer: Lord Jesus, help me to discover my gifts early and teach me
how to bless the world with them.

Jesus says: You are the Light of the world!
Your borders shall not be limited.
When you travel afar, Jesus will be just a
call away.
The Good Shepherd will hold your hand
every step of the way.

Take little steps of faith, and great doors
will open for you.
Wherever your feet land, they will carry
blessings.
You shall escape every trap of darkness.
Like a lamp, Jesus' Word will guide your
path ahead, always.

Prayer: Dear Lord Jesus, light my path wherever I go.
May I bring honor to Your name always.

Jesus says: You are the Light of the world!
The whole world is your stage,
They wait to see your star shine.
So arise! Let your light shine, for the
world to see
The glory of the Lord Jesus, perfectly
displayed in you.

Whenever you call, Jesus will send helpers
from near and far.
He will never leave you alone or reject you.
When you walk through life's fire, it will not
burn you.
His angels will watch over you, my little angel.

Prayer: Dear Lord Jesus, send me helpers whenever I am down, out, or stuck.

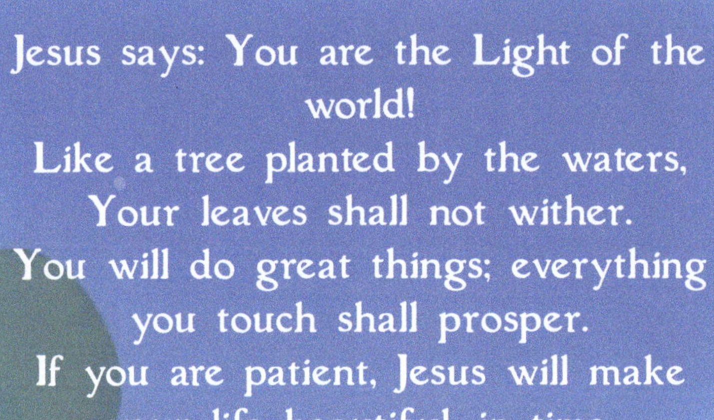

Jesus says: You are the Light of the
world!
Like a tree planted by the waters,
Your leaves shall not wither.
You will do great things; everything
you touch shall prosper.
If you are patient, Jesus will make
your life beautiful, in time.

Jesus loves you dearly—just the way
you are.
Always remember that you are
special.
God's grace is enough to keep you
through life's battles.
You shall weather every storm and
emerge stronger each time.

Prayer: Dear Lord Jesus, keep me rooted in You, my source, that I may never run dry.

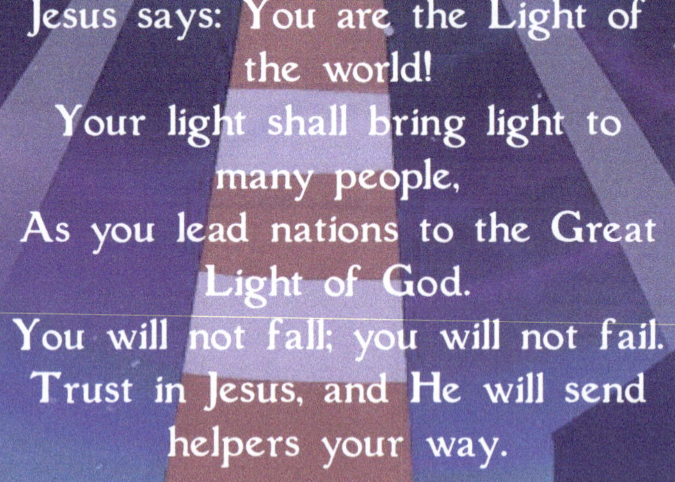

Jesus says: You are the Light of
the world!
Your light shall bring light to
many people,
As you lead nations to the Great
Light of God.
You will not fall; you will not fail.
Trust in Jesus, and He will send
helpers your way.

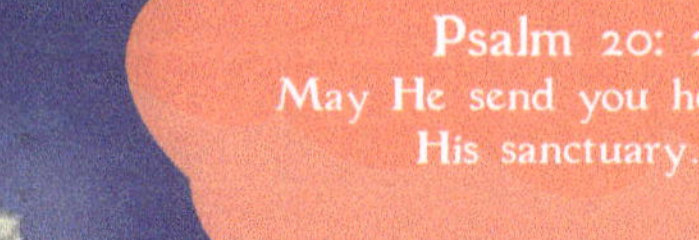

If you lose your way, Jesus will
carry you on Eagle's wings
And bring you back home to
Himself.
His goodness and mercy shall
follow you
All the days of your life.
Jesus will stay with you, forever.
Amen.

Prayer: Dear Lord Jesus, may Your blessings and mercy be with me, always.

I love you dearly, my darling. I pray
for you continually.
Jesus has crowned your head with
wisdom and grace.
Like Jesus, may you grow in
wisdom and favor.
Songs of joy and victory shall
forever be on your lips.

May your light shine brighter with
each passing day.
In your moments of weakness, Jesus
will give you grace.
May God's grace strengthen you as
you journey through Earth,
Until you make it home to heaven...
someday.

Good night, my darling. I love you so!
Sweet dreams, my little angel.

May the Lord Jesus be with you,
And bless you, always.
In Jesus' name, we pray. Amen.

Inspired by Grace Nkahnui.
In remembrance of Mami, Grace
Azenui. Your legacy lives on.
Forever in our hearts.